For Hal, Leo, Ruby and Siwan

Published in Great Britain in 2012
by Simon and Schuster UK Ltd
1st Floor, 222 Gray's Inn Road, London, WC1X 8HB
A CBS Company

A CIP catalogue record for this book is available
from the British Library upon request

ISBN: 978 0 85707 313 6 (HB)
ISBN: 978 0 85707 314 3 (PB)
ISBN: 978 0 85707 709 7 (eBook)

Printed in China
1 3 5 7 9 10 8 6 4 2

How Dinosaurs Really Work!

by Alan Snow

SIMON AND SCHUSTER
London New York Sydney Toronto New Delhi

THE TERRIBLE LIZARDS!

or not . . .

There was a time long ago when dinosaurs ruled the Earth. Dinosaurs were prehistoric reptiles. The word DINOSAUR comes from two Greek words – DEINOS which means terrible, powerful or wondrous, and SAUROS which means lizard. So they could be called TERRIBLE LIZARDS - except that, in fact, not all were terrible and none were lizards.

Dinosaurs were beasts of many shapes, sizes and types, and they were closely related to modern birds.

Some were meat-eating monsters whilst others were plant-eating creatures.

Oi! Are you our cousin?

Triassic Period
250–205 million years ago

Jurassic Period
205–144 million years ago

Cretaceous Period
144–65 million years ago

Terrible vegetarian dinosaurs attacking pre-historic giant carrots (which probably didn't exist).

Dinosaurs didn't exist when your parents were young so attacks on the way to school were not a problem.

So when DID the dinosaurs rule the Earth? Well, you know that your parents are old – dinosaurs are much, MUCH older than that. Even when your grandparents were young, there were no dinosaurs. The first dinosaurs appeared about 230 million years ago and all the dinosaurs died out around 65 million years ago.

Humans have only been around for about 200,000 years.

I love jumping queues!

Oi, I was here first.

Tertiary Period
63–1.8 million years ago

You lot! Fancy a burger?

Dinosaurs lived on the planet for about 165 million years (which is about 800 times longer than us humans have been here).

He's heavy! We've used ten tons of clay already!

Our picture of what dinosaurs look like comes mostly from fossils. These were made by dead dinosaurs being trapped in mud and slowly buried. Over time, the soft parts rotted away, but the bones turned to stone. Dinosaur fossils are very rare so we may never know the shapes and types of ALL dinosaurs.

When early fossils were discovered, people often didn't know which part of the dinosaur they had found. One man thought he had found a horn from a dinosaur's nose but he had actually found its thumb!

This one would have made a good pet.

Help! I'm sinking.

Hold on! We'll get you out.

4

you think Bill, is it a leg?

know George, it could be an arm.

Mary Anning was one of the greatest early fossil hunters. She discovered the first ichthyosaur when she was only 12 years old.

As WHOLE dinosaur fossils were discovered, people studied them and tried to imagine how the complete creature would look. Today, palaeontologists (people who study fossils and the nature of dinosaurs) spend a lot of time modelling dinosaurs on computers so we can work out how they would have moved.

We still don't know for sure what colour dinosaurs were but we can guess that they might have needed camouflage, or markings to attract a mate – or even to scare off other dinosaurs!

Green suits him!

Shall we add more belly? He looks a bit skinny.

Mary, stop digging up the garden!

But look, Dad!

I like the red one.

Oh no, I love purple.

STEGOSAURUS (STEG-uh-SAWR-us)

Stegosaurus means Roof Lizard

The Stegosaurus was a large dinosaur with seventeen big, sharp protective plates on its back, and spikes that were over a metre long on its tail. If it was attacked, it was definitely a fighter rather than a runner-away!

Mashed salad again!

What's for lunch?

Aargh! Why aren't you running away from me?

DINO FACTS
WEIGHT: 3 TONNES
HEIGHT: 4 METRES
LENGTH: 9 METRES

There have been some weird theories about the Stegosauru One theory is that they had two brains – one in its head and the other in its behind.

I'll have the salad with a side order of rocks please.

Of course, Sir.

The Stegosaurus' tail is called a thagomizer. The cartoonist Gary Larson did a cartoon about a Stegosaurus bashing a caveman with his tail.

The Stegosaurus was a plant-eating creature. It had a beak and small teeth so it couldn't chew its food. Instead, it would swallow plants and then, in its tummy, rocks (that it had also swallowed!) would move around and mash up the plants.

The Stegosaurus' head was about the same size as a cow's head but its brain was about the same size as a rabbit's!

The caveman was called Thag Simmons, hence the word 'thagomize'.

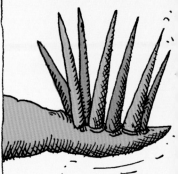

And what are you implying exactly?

WALKIES!

DINO JOKE

What do you call a plated dinosaur when he's asleep?

StegoSNOREus

Take your partner by the hand.

Another Stegosaurus theory is that it walked on two legs

TRICERATOPS (try-SAIR-uh-tops)

Triceratops means
Three-horned Face

1
2
3

I'm
cool man.

Too
high!

Triceratops was a three-horned dinosaur with a huge protective plate over its head. It had one of the largest skulls of any land-dwelling animal. Triceratops would have used its head to defend itself and to attract mates. Its head may even have helped it to keep cool! It seems that, despite having this protective armour, Triceratops didn't charge at things as its skull may have been too delicate.

Triceratops may have lived in herds and was somewhat like a modern-day rhino but they are not related (except in a very, very, VERY distant way).

Empty the
waste.

Hurry up!

More fu
needed

DINO FACTS
WEIGHT: 8 TONNES
HEIGHT: 3 METRES
LENGTH: 9 METRES

Triceratops ate ferns and
other low-growing plants.

Aha!
Just right.

Oi!
Are you
my cousin?

Don't hurt yourself.

Run for it!

DINO JOKE

What do you get if you cross a Triceratops with a kangaroo?

Tricera-HOPS

Triceratops lived at the same time as Tyrannosaurus Rex but it wasn't as bright as T. rex. In fact, it wasn't even as bright as a crocodile!

Triceratops reproduced by laying eggs. There's a lot palaeontologists still don't know about dinosaurs. For example was the Torosaurus a grown-up Triceratops or a completely different species of dinosaur?

That's my egg!

I want to be a Torosaurus too.

NO, am not!

You may be!

APATOSAURUS (ah-PAT-uh-SAWR-us)
aka BRONTOSAURUS

Translation for Apatosaurus is Deceptive Lizard

The Apatosaurus is more commonly known as the Brontosaurus and existed about 150 million years ago. It was one of the largest land animals that has ever lived – although not as big as its lesser-known relative, the Supersaurus, which was as long as four buses! The longest Apatosaurus was only as long as two buses but weighed as much as three or four elephants.

DINO FACTS
WEIGHT: 30 TONNES
HEIGHT: 9 METRES
LENGTH: 20 METRES

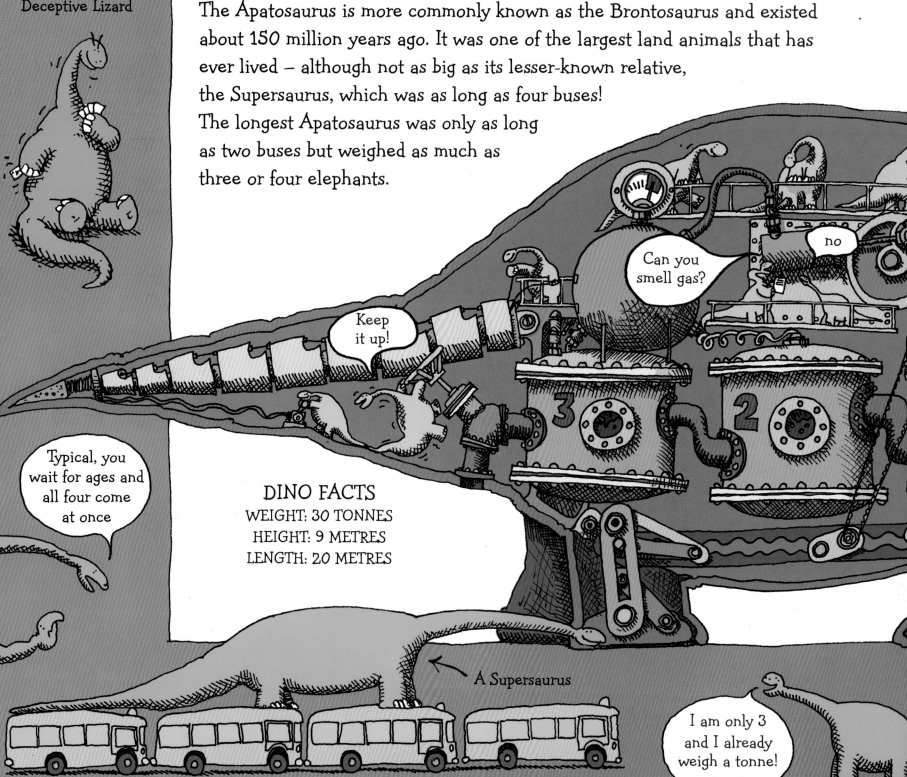

A Supersaurus

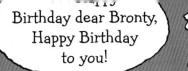

Birthday dear Bronty,
Happy Birthday
to you!

It grew incredibly quickly and reached full size by the time it was ten years old. It had an extremely long neck (around 6 metres long) with a rather small head. Its brain was probably the size of a big apple. It would have used its long tail to defend itself. One scientist believes that, when the Apatosaurus cracked its tail like a whip, it probably made a noise as loud as a cannon!

Whee!

What a pain in the neck!

DINO JOKE

What's worse than a
giraffe with a sore throat?

An Apatosaurus with a sore throat.

Feed me!

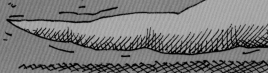

VELOCIRAPTOR (Veh-loss-ih-RAP-tor)

Velociraptor means
Rapid Robber

Velociraptor is one of the well-known small, predatory dinosaurs. About the size of a turkey, the Velociraptor is nonetheless said to be a cunning and calculating meat-eater. It is believed that this dinosaur hunted in groups, not unlike many carnivorous animals today, such as wolves and lions.

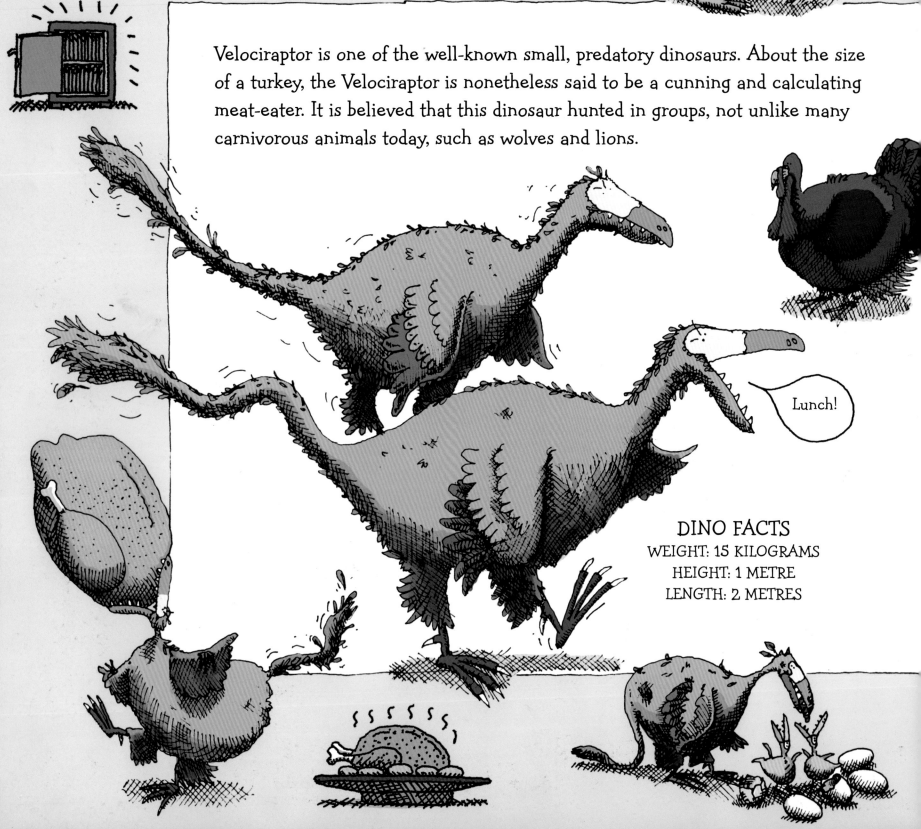

Lunch!

DINO FACTS
WEIGHT: 15 KILOGRAMS
HEIGHT: 1 METRE
LENGTH: 2 METRES

Recently, scientists discovered some evidence that the Velociraptor may have been feathered. This helps to prove the theory that birds descended from the dinosaurs, and that the feathers came first, before the bird's ability to fly.

DINO JOKE

What happened when the dinosaur took the train home?

He had to bring it back!

(tye-RAN-uh-SAWR-us)

Tyrannosaurus
means
Tyrant Lizard.
Rex means King

Tyrannosaurus Rex is often known by its nickname of T. rex. It was one of the biggest carnivores (meat-eaters) that has ever lived and weighed more than four small cars. Its jaws were so strong that it would probably have been able to chomp down on a medium-sized tree. However, it probably wouldn't have ever done so as this dinosaur DEFINITELY preferred tasty meat. It could eat 250 kilos of meat in one bite!
It is thought to have lived by hunting and scavenging for dead animals.

Its head was almost two metres long but it had very small arms. In fact, its arms were so small that they couldn't even reach its mouth! Some scientists believe that T. rex could run at speeds of 45 mph (but was probably rubbish at turning corners when going fast).
The biggest tooth from one ever found was bigger than a man's foot.

Keep the
tail balanced.

I am
getting
tired.

Oh, no!
Missed the
corner again!

Look out,
corner!

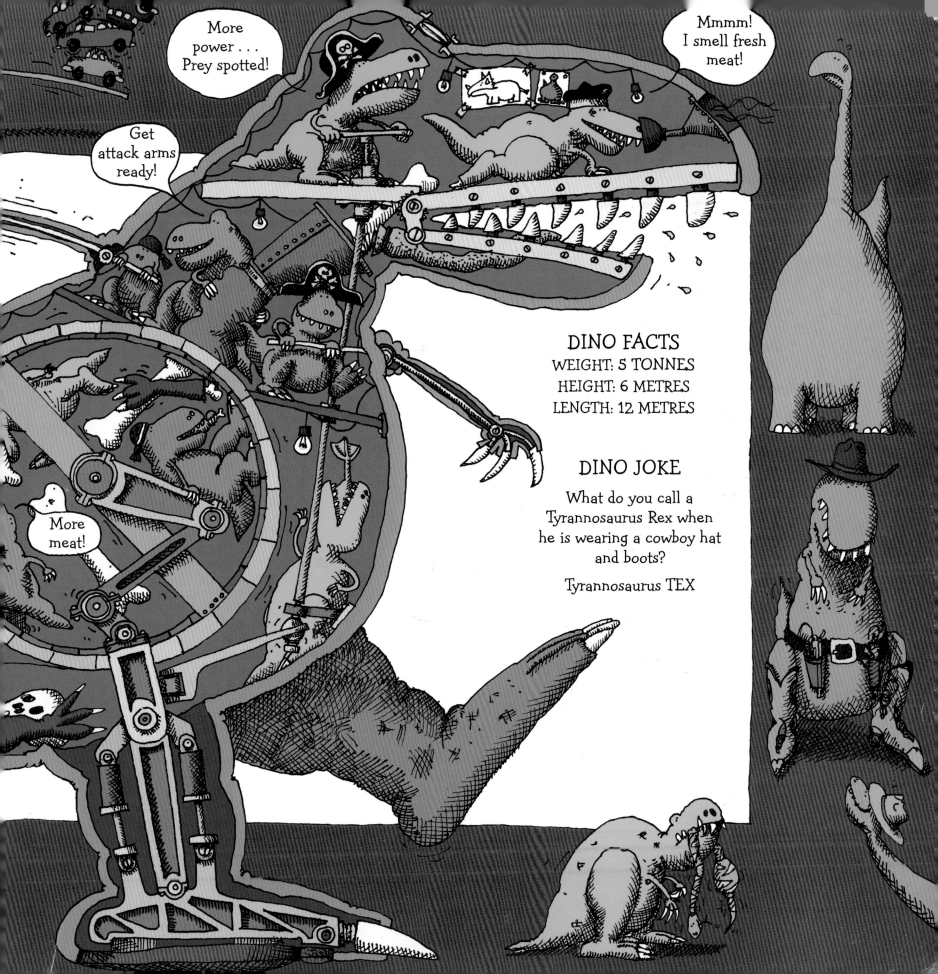

T. REX BRAIN

HOW DID IT THINK?

DINO JOKE

Why don't dinosaurs ever forget?

Because they never knew anything in the first place!

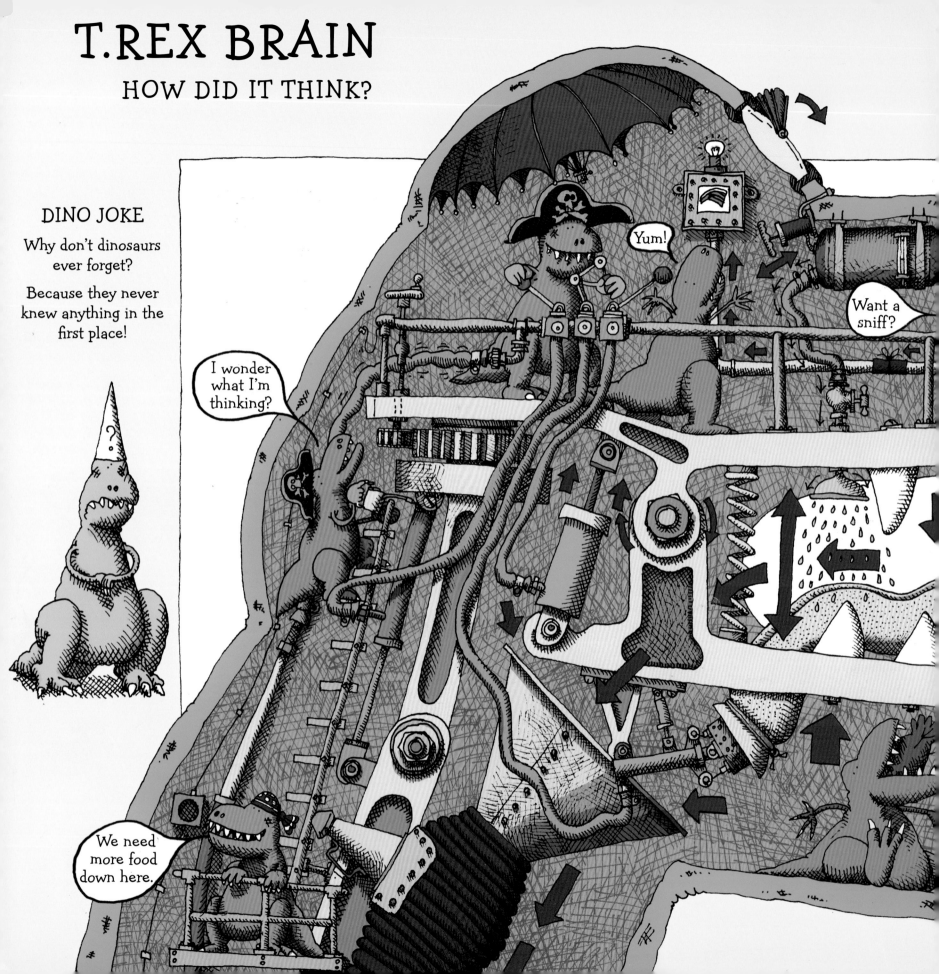

Fig. 1

Fig. 2

Fig. 3

Fig. 4

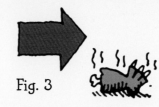

T. rex was not the cleverest of creatures but it was not completely stupid. It had a fantastic sense of smell and would have been able to sniff out rotting dead animals from a long way away, and live animals from almost as far. Its brain was bigger than that of most other dinosaurs and about the same size as a human brain, but the bit that did the clever thinking was much smaller. Many of its thoughts were very simple and probably went something like this:

Fig. 5

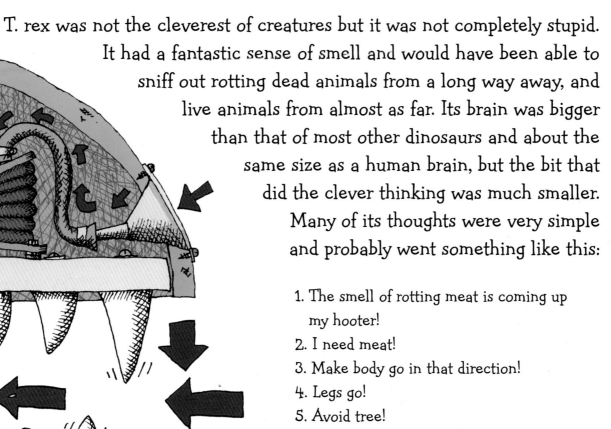

1. The smell of rotting meat is coming up my hooter!
2. I need meat!
3. Make body go in that direction!
4. Legs go!
5. Avoid tree!
6. Eyes look for dead thing!
7. I see something that looks dead and the smell is really niffy
8. Open jaws
9. Bend down
10. Chomp!
11. YUM!

Fig. 6

Fig. 7

Fig. 11

Fig. 10

Fig. 9

Fig. 8

Who wants to be a dinosaur anyway!

Though there are lots of well-known dinosaurs, some of the less well-known are just as interesting, and many were pretty weird . . .

PTEROSAURS

Pterosaurs were flying reptiles. The largest pterosaur of all time (Quetzalcoatlus) had a wingspan of about 15 metres – longer than a double-decker bus!

PROTOCERATOPS

Unearthed skeletons of this beaked dinosaur may have been the source of the myth of the Griffin.

PACHYCEPHALOSAURUS

This dinosaur defended itself with its thick skull.

I'm a legend!

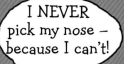

– yummy!

THERIZINOSAURUS
This vegetarian dinosaur had huge claws that were about one metre in length.

CARNOTAURUS
This dinosaur had arms so short that they were little more than stumps.

I NEVER pick my nose – because I can't!

DINO JOKE
What do you call a dinosaur that picks its nose and eats it?

Disgusting!

JEHOLOPTERUS
It was once thought that this small, hairy pterosaur may have attached itself to large dinosaurs and sucked their blood – imagine a prehistoric vampire!

Don't tell anyone we are related!

TSINTAOSAURUS SPINORHINUS
This dinosaur had a bill like a duck and a horn like a unicorn.

ROAR!

There are many theories as to why dinosaurs died out. Here are some of them:

1. Either a comet hit the Earth or a huge volcanic eruption caused such a large cloud of dust in the atmosphere that it completely changed the weather, making it grow much colder or hotter.

2. Changes to Earth's temperatures and sea levels destroyed the dinosaurs' habitats.

3. New diseases, probably carried by insects, infected them.

4. New and more successful creatures evolved and the dinosaurs couldn't compete with them.

Someone turn the tap off!

Yum, this is eggcellent!

Brrr! It's cold.

DINO JOKE

Why did the dinosaur go extinct?

Because he wouldn't have a bath!

DINOSAURS TODAY

DINO JOKE

What do you get if you cross a crocodile with a flower?

I don't know, but I'm not going to smell it!

There are still dinosaurs today (or at least very close relations!)

CROCODILES

Crocodiles are not (and were never) pure dinosaurs but they lived at the same time. They were probably not as bright as some dinosaurs – which just goes to show that you don't necessarily need to be bright to succeed.

SHARKS

Sharks first appeared about 400 million years ago, long before the first dinosaurs. Megalodon was the largest shark that ever lived. It was about the same size as a humpback whale and its jaws were so large it could have swallowed a cow whole!

I love burgers!

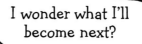

I wonder what I'll become next?

THE GIANT MOA

This massive flightless bird, native to New Zealand, died out about 500 years ago. It was an extremely fierce creature, with sharp talons and a very strong beak.

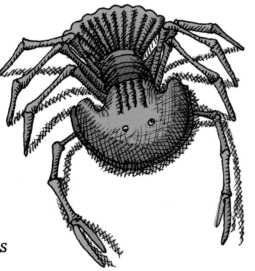

CRABS and TURTLES

Horse-shoe crab fossils have been found that are half a billion years old.

Turtles lived as long ago as a quarter of a billion years.

SEA URCHINS

Sea Urchins existed even before dinosaurs!

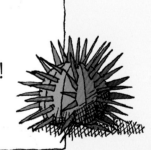

HOW TO BUILD A WOOLLY MAMMOTH

(Please note: not actually a dinosaur!)

The Woolly Mammoth, a mammal, was not really a dinosaur but a distant relation of the elephant. They lived from about 1 million years ago and died out around three and a half thousand years ago (long after the invention of beer and ice skating!). They are often found frozen in ice in Siberia.

SMALL EARS SO AS NOT TO LOOSE HEAT THROUGH THEM

THREE LAYERS OF HAIR TO KEEP THE COLD OUT

To make a woolly mammoth, you might perhaps do the following:

- Get one full-size Asian elephant
- Wrap it in enough padding to keep out the bitter Arctic cold
- Extend its tusks so it can dig through the snow and find things to eat
- Hide enough buns under the snow for it to find
- Try and keep the elephant happy!

MAMMOTH JOKE

Why did the woolly mammoth cross the road?

Because there were no chickens in the Ice Age!